The Holy Men

Mandela Addah

Ukiyoto Publishing

Contents

The Holy Men

Sandra Johnson was a twenty-two-year-old African Canadian woman who lived in Edmonton, Alberta. That afternoon she was seated in the rear section of a city bus. Sandra was busy reading a good courtroom drama novel. The city bus was grey and blue, as were all of the busses and streetcars found in Edmonton. Sandra was going to her university campus. She had recently eaten lunch at a nearby restaurant with her long-time boyfriend Sebastian. Sebastian was a medical student that attended Sandra's university. Sebastain was a foreign student. He originated from the African country called Ghana.

Sandra was a religious woman. She was also a full-time student at The University of Alberta. She wanted to get a position as a religion teacher at a Catholic high school after graduating from university in a month's time. Sandra stood exactly five feet. She had an average figure and puffy black hair that was not an afro. That day she was wearing a large blue and black backpack. She also wore a blouse and blue jeans.

Her backpack was filled with textbooks and school supplies.

That day there were twelve other people that were

seated on the same bus she was. They were all doing their own thing and minding their own business. Eventually the bus arrived at one of Edmonton's many subway stations. The subway station had eight concrete stairs that led downstairs into a wide-open area where the ticket booth could be found. Past the ticket booths were more stairs that led downstairs to the subway tracks. Sandra left the city bus. Sandra hastily made her down the concrete stairs. She did not want to be late for her professor's lecture. Her professor did not likethat.

Sandra was in a little too much of a hurry. She clumsily tripped over her own two feet and she painfully fell down the eight concrete stairs, smashing her left knee on the concrete ground. Sandra rolled around on the ground in pain. She had just broken her left knee.

A Chinese man that was walking down the stairs behind her immediately came to her aid. He had short black hair, wore dress pants and had a short sleeve blue dress shirt. He crouched to her side.

"What happened?" He asked.

"My knee." Said Sandra in great pain. "I just broke my left knee."

There was an overweight woman inside the toll booth where subway fare was paid. There was also another ticket agent to her opposite side. The woman was Caucasian, she had short black hair and wore round glasses. She also wore a professional looking subway employee uniform. The ticket agent woman could tell that something bad had happened. She left her small booth and quickly came to Sandra's aid. Some people in the train station stopped to look at her while others past by and did not get involved.

"What happened here?" Asked the subway employee woman.

The Chinese man stood upright to face her. "This poor woman just fell down these concrete stairs and she broke her knee." The woman looked down at Sandra, then back up at the Chinese man. "I will call for an ambulance." She said. The woman then pulled her cell phone out and dialed 911.

Ten minutes later, a red and white ambulance arrived at the subway stations entrance. Two paramedics came down the concrete stairs that led downstairs and into the subway station, and they carried a folded white cot with them. Both paramedics were wearing professional looking light blue uniforms. The first paramedic was a tall well-built man. He had short curly blonde hair, the second was a woman. She had long black hair in a ponytail, and they both wore white latex gloves. The female paramedic fell to one knee in front of Sandra. Sandra was still on the ground on her back and was still in a bit of pain. "Whathappened here?" Asked the woman paramedic.

Then the Chinese man then explained to the woman paramedicabout what had recently happened.

Both paramedics gently lifted Sandra, and they gently

placed her on the cot that lay on the ground to her left side. Then they both raised its ends, and carried her up the eight concrete stairs that she had recently fallen down. When they got to the surface they loaded Sandra into the open rear doors of the ambulance, then the doors were closed shut. Then the ambulance the drove off to the nearest hospital.

Chapter 1

A few hours later. An orange and white taxi cab pulled up to The University of Edmonton's campus in front of Sandra's apartment building. The campus had all kinds of different sized buildings. Quite a few of them held classrooms and lecture halls, while others were meant to house its many students. Sandra paid the taxi cab driver, and then he drove away. She then limped away in the opposite direction. Sandra now wore a white brace over her broken left knee, and she would be forced to limp around the university campus on crutches. Crutches that the hospital had kindly given her, and Sandra was still wearing her backpack.

Sandra went to her apartment building. Getting around campus on crutches was cumbersome, and it would take some serious getting used to. That Friday afternoon, Sandra sat inside one of her university's many lecture halls. She took down notes as her professor made her lecture. Fifty other students were seated in the lecture hall that day. Different students sat in different rows, and to the front of the lecture hall was a wide chalkboard.

In front of the blackboard stood the woman professor. She was wearing a black blouse and a long dress, and was making her lecture. Tuning out her professor for a moment, Sandra rubbed her left knee. It still hurt a bit after falling down the concrete stairs at the city'ssubway system a few days prior.

An hour later the lecture had ended. Her professor had mentioned that all of her students had to write a major paper on world religions as part of their final grade. Sandra put on her knapsack, and she grabbed her crutches that were to her side. Then Sandra limped out of the lecture hall, and she went back to her residence building. Her small apartment could be found on the second floor of a twelve-story residence building, the building was built of large dark brown brick. It also had windows on all sides, and Sandra lived alone.

After catching the elevator to the second floor, Sandra pulled out her key card. She used it to open her apartment door, and went inside. Sandra sat on her small bed. Her small apartment came with one small bed, a bathroom, and a small narrow kitchen. It also held a microwave and cupboards on both sides above the microwave holding different dishes. She also had a desk in the bedroom, where her desktop computer was, and a shelf that was filled with more text books. There was also a wide window in her bedroom that peered out at the University campus.

Now Sandra had to write a major book report on world religions, and her knee injury was only going to slow her down. Sandra sat on her bed. She usually knelt in order to pray. Though doing that would only aggravate her broken knee. She closed her eyes and she prayed to God. She asked him to help her write her report on world religions. After praying she laid on her bed and closed her eyes. She would go to the university library tomorrow, and tomorrow was Saturday.

Chapter 2

Sandra awoke Saturday morning. She yawned, stretched and she hopped on one foot into her bedroom. After taking a nice hot shower, she put on some blue jeans, a comfortable cotton shirt, and running shoes. Sandra would find some food in the university's cafeteria, and the cafeteria was open for business every day.

The university food court had twenty different tables inside. It also had a wide-open window to the rear that peered out at the university campus. There were five different restaurants. The first sold pizza, the second sold donuts, the third sold submarine sandwiches, the fourth sold hamburgers, while the fifth sold fried chicken. Sandra paid for three pieces of fried chicken, some fries and a cola. A kind fellow student helped her carry her food to the nearest table. She politely thanked him, then placed her backpack on the ground to her side along with her crutches. She then sat down and began to eat her fried chicken. One minute later, a lone man walked into the cafeteria. He glanced around until he saw Sandra. He then smiled and walked up to her.

He looked down at her. "Excuse me? May I sit here?" He asked. "Go ahead." She glanced up at him, then resumed eating her fried chicken. The man then sat down facing her.

The man seated across from Sandra was in his mid-thirties, and was well dressed. He wore a black suit with a black dress shirt and a black tie. He had nicely trimmed short hair and wore a digital watch. He also had a slightly darker skin tone, though he was not African or East Indian. Sandra wasn't sure what his nationality was. He glanced down at her food he then looked back up at her. "You know, that stuff will kill you." "Excuse me?" She asked, looking up at him, confused. "That stuff will kill you." He repeated. "That sugary cola, and thatgreasy fried chicken."

Sandra paused for a second before replying. "Do I know you?" He smiled at her. "Now you do. My name is Jesus Christ." Sandra closed her eyes and she sighed deeply. It was just her luck to have caught the attention of this idiot that was either mentally ill or a Jehovah's Witness. "I'm not interested." She tried to say politely. The man seated across from her looked shocked. "I'm not here to sell you anything!" He said. "I've just come to answer your prayer." Sandra had no tolerance or patience for people like this. "Excuse me." She said. Sandra got to her feet and she left University cafeteria using her crutches, leaving her unfinished fried chicken and unfinished drink on the cafeteria table. She hoped that she would never run into that stupid man again. Sandra limped back to her apartment building. Then she caught the elevator to her second-floor level and went into her apartment using her key card. Then she closed and locked the door behind her. When she turned around, she bumped into the same man that she had just met in the university cafeteria!

Sandra took one step backwards; then she lost her balance and fell hard against the back of her door then dropped down to her buttocks. Pain flared through her broken knee, and her two crutches fell to her side. Sandra was now trapped inside her apartment with some weirdo! How did he get into her apartment? How did he know where she lived? Had he been stalking her? What if he was a pervert?

"If you don't get out of my apartment right now, I'll scream!" She warned him. Then the man raised his left hand and suddenly Sandra felt nothing but peace and calm. She somehow knew that this strange man would not harm her. He fell to one knee facing her, then he gently placed his open palms on opposite sides of Sandra's broken knee, a second later the pain was gone. The man who claimed to be Jesus stood, he smiled, extended his hand and pulled Sandra to her feet. Without saying a word, Sandra knew that she could take off her knee brace. She then lifted her left knee. Flexing it freely and moving it without feeling any pain or discomfort. Jesus had really healed her! She took one step back and she looked at him, amazed. "You're Jesus Christ?" "I am." He replied, crossing his arms, and smiling at her. Sandra was not sure what to say next. She was still having trouble thinking that she was really speaking face to face with the Son of God. "If you're Jesus Christ, what are you doing in my university apartment?"

"God sent me to answer your prayer. "He replied. "I on't understand?" She asked, confused. "Last night you prayed and you asked God to help you write your report on world religions." He said. "So, God decided to send a holy man representing each of the world's six major religions to speak with you face to face. We will answer all of your questions and teach you about our fantastic religions." "Wow." Exclaimed Sandra.

Jesus raised a finger. "But know this, we will only answer your questions, we will not write your report for you. After hearing all six of us out, and having answered all of your questions, you can write your report. Do you understand?" "I think so." Replied Sandra, bewildered. Jesus took her arm and led her out the door. She looked at him strangely. "Where are you taking me?" Jesus smiled and gently pulled her along. "We're going to have atalk, a very long talk."

Chapter 3

Sandra and Jesus left her apartment building and went into one of the universities many school buildings. They walked down a wide hallway and then they sat on a wide wooden bench found against the wall. Quite a few students walked past them in both directions, up and down the wide-open hallway.

"Aren't people listening?" She asked, looking around uncomfortably. Jesus laid back on the bench. "Not really." "I could have never thought that my prayer would be answered like this." She said. "The Father likes to work in mysterious ways." Replied Jesus. Then Sandra asked Jesus her first religion-based question. "What does God look like, and where does God come from?" Jesus shook his head. "Forgive me Sandra. But I cannot speak of such things." "How come?" She asked.

"Because the Father told me, and the other five holy men that we were not to describe his physical appearance or his origins." He replied. "That is why The Father's physical appearance or his true origins were never mentioned in the Bible. Pardon me Sandra but I have to respect The Father's wishes and his privacy." Sandra knew that Jesus meant God whenever he used the word Father, and she did not appreciate him contradicting her. "Shouldn't you have a full beard and long brown hair?" Asked Sandra.

Jesus smiled as he rubbed his chin with his right hand. "Nah, nowadays I prefer the clean-cut look." "Shouldn't you be wearing a robe?" She asked. Jesus shook his head. "I'm afraid they're out of fashion." Sandra moistened her lips before speaking again. "Why does God put us here on Earth in the first place?" "It's all part of the test." Replied Jesus. "And everyone in the world serves their own purpose." "What test?" Asked Sandra, confused.

"Life is one big test." Repeated Jesus. "Everyone is given a series of choices to make. You can be kind or you can be cruel. You can be wise or you can be a fool. You can be honest or you can be dishonest. You can work hard or you can be lazy. You can steal or you can choose not to steal. You can be generous or you can be greedy, or you can be brave or you can be a coward. The day you die, the test is over. The Father will not simply let you into Heaven, you have to earn your place there, and everyone is responsible for their own destiny." Sandra made an odd face. "If God gives us all free will, why does God give guys the choice to be jerks?" Jesus laughed softly. "It's all part of the test, and jerks make the world a more interesting place." Sandra was confused. "Then why doesn't God just come down and make himself known instead of being mysterious and unseen?" Jesus shook his head. "Because Sandra, some things aren't meant to be proven." Sandra spoke again. "There are some things I never understood. Some people are deeply religious, yet they end up getting killed in a car crash or something. Why does God allow that?"

"People don't die at random Sandra." Explained Jesus. "The Father selects a time and place for us all. Those people all died because their time had come." "Then how come sometimes deeply religious people end up getting Cancer or something for no good reason. Why does God allow that?" She asked. Jesus looked across the hallway. "Because during final judgement The Father will compensate us for all for all of the pain, suffering and injustice that we went through when we were alive. You see all of those good people who get sick with Cancer or some kind of terminal disease, they're the lucky ones. Because one day The Father will compensate them for all their suffering." "Secondly, Sandra. Cancer does not discriminate. Anybody can get Cancer at any time." He said. "Cancer doesn't care if you're religious, it doesn't care if you're kind, it doesn't care what you look like, it doesn't care if you're rich, it doesn't care if you're a celebrity. It doesn't care if you are a doctor, The Pope, or The President of the United States. No one is safe from Cancer, nobody." Sandra hesitated before changing the subject again. "Is there really a Devil?"

"Oh, he's very real." Replied Jesus. "And his goal is to take souls away from the Father, and his objective is the downfall of all mankind." "Then what is Satan like in real life?" She asked. Jesus shook his head again. "He's really complicated." Sandra repeated herself. "Then what is Satan like in real life, exactly?" Jesus thought to himself for another second before replying. "Satan is evil, cruel, ruthless, cunning, clever, mysterious, patient, scheming, he's a charismatic leader and he's highly intelligent." "Then what is Satan's true form?" Asked Sandra. Jesus looked across the hallway again. "A great and terrible beast." Sandra spoke again. "Can you really sell your soul to the Devil?" "Yes, you can." Confirmed Jesus. Jesus continued. "You see something Sandra, Satan can only tempt you to sin but he cannot force you to sin." Sandra was confused again. "Why is that?" Jesus looked at her. "Because if Satan forces you to sin, then you are not at fault, and he gains nothing." That also made sense.

Sandra spoke again. "It was written in the book of Matthew that Satan tempted you in the desert. He offered you all of the kingdoms of the world if you were to simply bow down and worship him. Yet you refused, may I ask why?" "Because Satan was lying to me about all of his proposals." Said Jesus. "And Satan is the father of lies." He spoke again. "You may not realize it Sandra, but one of Satan's greatest accomplishments is convincing us that he doesn't exist. He actually prefers that we don't believe in him." Sandra made another odd face. "That doesn't make any sense." "Actually, it does." Replied Jesus. "Those who have no belief in a Devil find it easier to sin." Sandra changed the subject yet again. "There is something else that I have always wondered about. I know that stealing is a sin. Let's say that some man sees great poverty in countless people and he dearly wants to help them out. So, he finds a way to steal ten million dollars from some big corporation and then he gives that ten million dollars to those countless poor people. Is he at fault?" "Yes, he is." Replied Jesus. "If that man wants to give money to the sick, poor and needy, he can give them his own hard-earned money, not someone else's." That also made a lot of sense.

She spoke again. "In the New Testament you mentioned that those who live by the sword die by the sword. Did you mean that people who live violent lives die violently?" "Of course." Said Jesus. "That especially applies to violent criminals. Drug dealers often get killed, people in street gangs often get killed, and people who are involved in organized crime or the Mafia often get killed. They live violently so they die violently." Sandra changed the subject again. "Why does God allow for so much suffering in the world? And why does God make good people suffer?" "Without the clouds how would we appreciate the sun?" Replied Jesus. "And whatever doesn't kill you only makes you stronger. When someone goes through a very hard time in their lives and that person survives. That person will emerge stronger and wiser. The more you suffer in your lifetime the stronger you become, and sometimes it takes something painful in order to make someone change their ways." Sandra changed the subject yet again. "The Bible says that you once walked on water. How do you explain that scientifically?"

Jesus shook his head. "You can't. God has power over science. It was recorded in the Bible that one day I came across a blind beggar that I pitied. So, I spat into the dirt and I turned that dirt into mud. Then I rubbed that mud onto both of the blind man's eyes. After the blind man had washed the mud off of his eyes in a nearby fountain his sight had been fully restored. Try explaining that in your science textbook." "What language did you speak when you first walked the Earth?" Asked Sandra. "Aramaic." He replied. Sandra changed the subject. "Why does God create diseases?" "In truth, he doesn't." Replied Jesus. "Diseases are part of nature. Just like earthquakes, tornadoes and floods." "Then why doesn't God use his divine intervention and make all fatal diseases go away?" She asked.

Jesus shook his head again. "Because Sandra, that would just exchange one problem for another. If there were no fatal diseases the world's population would be many times higher. As a result, the planet would be over crowded, there wouldn't be enough food to go around and everyone would starve. Tell me, would that be any better?" "Then what is Hell like?" Asked Sandra. Changing the subject yet again. "In The New Testament you often mentioned it." Jesus became very serious. "Hell is a very real place Sandra, and it is the one place that you don't ever want to go. It is far worse than any nightmare or horror movie. Crying, screaming, suffering, agony, and people's souls being horribly tortured by demons. People getting their flesh ripped off, It's horrendous, and Hell stinks." She spoke again. "Then where is Hell?" "Hell can be found in the center of the planet." Replied Jesus. "The Bible confirms that." Sandra didn't understand. "How could such a loving God create a Hell?"

Jesus frowned. "People create their own Hell Sandra, and no one ends up in Hell by accident. Say there is an evil man that tortures, and brutally murders twelve children? What is The Father supposed to do with people that choose to be so evil? Those who are evil and corrupt can change their ways at any time, and there is always great joy in Heaven when an evil and corrupt person turns their backs to evil and develops a faith." Then why doesn't God just remove evil from people?" She asked. "That way no one would end up in Hell?"

"Because that would mean that The Father would force people to be good." Replied Jesus. "And The Father will never force us to do something against our will, and you cannot force someone to be religious. If someone chooses to pursue a faith, it must be a decision that that person makes for themselves, and if someone seeks forgiveness for any sin they may have committed they need only ask for it, and The Father will always forgive them." She changed the subject again. "In the New Testament you said that everyone dies and faces final judgement. What happens during finaljudgement?"

"The day you die, your soul will leave your body, and this world forever." Replied Jesus. "Your soul then meets God face to face. Then you will have to answer to him for all of the choices that you made when you were on Earth. The Father will let you know why you suffered the way you did during your lifetime. Then he will compensate you for all of the pain, suffering and injustice that you may have gone through when you were alive." "I'll be rich." Exclaimed Sandra.

Jesus ignored her remark and continued. "As far as The Father is concerned, no good deed goes unrewarded and no sin will go unpunished. In the end, everybody will get exactly what they deserve, no more, no less, and no one will get away with anything, and if you are a good person, the day you die is better than the day you are born." "How long does final judgement take?" Asked Sandra. Jesus smiled at her. "Final judgement will happen in less than a blink of an eye."

He continued. "Also, if someone had committed a serious sin when they were alive and that person paid for it in prison. The Father will also take that into consideration." Sandra spoke again. "Let's say there is a very good person who does not believe in a God. How will God judge such a person?" Jesus happily explained. "When that individual dies and their soul meets God face to face, they'll change their opinions real fast." "Another thing." He said. "There is no such thing as an accidental sin. If someone commits a sin, a sin is always deliberate, you cannot sin by accident." Sandra addressed him yet again. "When you first walked the Earth, did you ever give money to street beggars?" "Not always." Replied Jesus. "Why is that?" She asked.

Jesus made himself more comfortable on the wooden bench before he replied. "Because Sandra, giving money to a street beggar can be unwise. That street beggar might take your money and use it to buy more drugs or more alcoholic drinks that will only make them worse. As far as street beggars go, the best thing you can do is pray for them. The Father knows what is best, and he can help them far better than your money can." He said smiling. "And best of all, it's free." "What about ghosts?" Asked Sandra. "What about them?" Replied Jesus. She looked Jesus in the eye. "Do ghosts exist?" Jesus had a blank expression on his face. "Yes, they do."

Sandra made another odd face. "But that doesn't make any sense, you just told me that when someone dies that they face final judgement. The Bible doesn't say anything about coming back as a ghost. What is a ghost supposed to be?" "A ghost is a someone whose soul is in limbo." Confirmed Jesus. "Their soul has not left this plane of existence because they have unfinished business in this world." "Then do ghosts ever hurt or attack people?" Asked Sandra. Jesus shook his head again. "Never, ghosts are harmless, though many people still fear them."

Sandra was confused. "But the Bible doesn't say anything about that." "We didn't want to confuse people." He replied. Sandra changed the subject yet again. "It is written in The Bible thatwhen good people die, their souls will go straight to Heaven. I don't understand, where is Heaven?" "It's in another realm." He explained. "Tell me more about Heaven?" She asked. "What is it like? It is the ultimate paradise." Said Jesus. "In Heaven there is no pain or suffering, and you don't have to work nine to five or go to school." Sandra spoke again. "Then what do people in Heaven eat?" Jesus shook his head again. "Nothing. Your soul does not need food Sandra, and your soul is immortal. It never gets old, never gets fat, and it never gets sick."

Jesus changed the subject. "There is another misinterpretation, that Satan is the supreme evil spirit. That is false. There are other evil supernatural beings that exist besides Satan, and people who study things like black magic are not necessarily Devil worshipers either." "Then you're saying that Voodoo practitioners are not Devil worshipers?" She asked. "Let me tell you something about Voodoo." Replied Jesus. "Voodoo is a very misunderstood religion. Voodoo is an ancient African religion that pre-dates Christianity by about six thousand years. Voodoo has been given a very bad reputation." "In truth, people that practice Voodoo are not evil. People who study Voodoo do not practice human sacrifice, and people that are into Voodoo are most certainly not Devil worshipers. In truth, Voodoo practitioners worship all kinds of different spirits, and deities, and they also believe in the existence of one supreme God whom they call Bondeye."

He continued. "If you were to watch enough movies involving Voodoo quite often, they mention the Voodoo doll. In the movie some Voodoo priest sticks needles or sharp objects into a Voodoo doll shaped after someone, and the person on the other end feels pain. There is no truth to that." He said. "The story of the Voodoo doll was something that Hollywood made up." "What about abortion?" She asked. "Are you against that?" "Of course, I am." Replied Jesus. "Abortion is murder, and it is a great and terrible evil. You're killing unborn children, what could be more evil than that? Every day in North America, countless women all over the country get abortions. Whenever a pregnant woman terminates her unborn child, it means that her child will never be brought into the world, never make friends, never go to school, never get a job, and will never contribute to society. It is a great and terrible loss." "That aborted child could have grown up into a doctor, a lawyer, a police officer, a judge, a politician, or maybe one day even cured a disease one day." "You see Sandra, a pregnant woman is a wonderful thing. It means that you're bringing new life into the world, and a baby is The Father's way of saying that the world must go on." Sandra spoke again. "Let's say a pregnant woman's doctor tells her that her child is going to be born retarded. Does that not justify an abortion?" "No, it does not." Replied Jesus "Why is that?" Asked Sandra. "Because Sandra." He said. If a child is born retarded, it is born retarded for a reason." Sandra didn't understand. "But that makes no sense.

What possible good can come from raising a retarded child?"

"You'd be surprised." Replied Jesus. "As I said earlier, The Father likes to work in mysterious ways. Perhaps raising a retarded child will teach the parents a valuable lesson, or maybe the retarded child will have a strong influence on others." Sandra changed the subject yet again. "The book of Genesis mentions The Garden of Eden. Where can The Garden of Eden be found?" Jesus held his jaw in his hand. "The Garden of Eden can be found somewhere in Iraq." "Then what happened to The Ark of the Covenant?" She asked. "Where is it now?" "It's hidden inside a church in somewhere in Ethiopia." He replied. She spoke again. "What part of the world did Noah's Ark take place?" "It took place in the country known as Turkey." He confirmed. Sandra was unsure. "When the great flood took place in The Old Testament, was it that part of the world that was flooded or was it the entire planet?" "It's difficult to say." Replied Jesus. "During Noah's time period Noah's part of the world was thought to be the entire planet." Sandra changed the subject. "Why doesn't the book of Genesis mention evolution?" "To be brutally honest." Said Jesus. "The Father really doesn't tell us too much. He never told us why it rains, why people get sick, or how a child is born. He left it for us to figure such things out for ourselves." She continued. "The Bible often speaks of angels. How many angels are there?" "About half a million." Replied Jesus. "Sandra changed the subject yet again. "If there is a God, why doesn't he help people? Why is our world in such disarray? Why doesn'tGod intervene?"

Jesus looked her in the eye. "Why don't you? One person can make a difference in the world. Look at people like Martin Luther King, Gandi, or Mother Teresa. I think it's sad when I hear so many people complaining about all of the world's problems, while they stand idly by and do nothing about it. Ordinary everyday people have the power to make a difference in the world by doing simple things such as helping others in need, or by giving money to different charities. I also find it sad when I see all those rich people who have more money that they know what to do with it. Yet they waste their money, buying things that they really don't need. They have the power to help countless people with their great riches, yet they sit on all of their money and let it accumulate. It is such a waste." Sandra changed the subject again. "The Bible speaks of your childhood. Then it speaks of you as an adult. What did you do in-between then? Where did you go?" He smiled at her. "I went to India and Tibet. When there I studied Buddhism and Hinduism." "How long does it take for our prayers to reach God?" She asked. Jesus snapped his fingers. "Just like that." "Then how does God hear our prayers?" Asked Sandra.

Jesus would also explain. "Whenever you stop to pray an invisible angel appears. That angel listens to all of your prayer then takes them straight The Father." Sandra changed the subject again. "In the past, there have been times when I had prayed for something, yet God did not answer. How do you explain that?" Jesus smiled at her. "Let me tell you three very short stories to help explain that." "One day there was an unemployed woman. She wanted to get a job at a nearby bank as a teller. Then she went to that bank, handed them her resume and had a job interview a few days later. She then prayed to God. She asked him to help her get the job. A few days later, the position went to another. That woman was very upset because she did not get the job position that she wanted so badly. Why hadn't God answer her prayers?" "The following day, that same woman was in her apartment reading the newspaper. According to the newspaper, the bank that she had recently applied to had been robbed, and several employees had been shot and killed. One of them was the same person who got the teller job."

Jesus continued. "During mid-December, there was a man. He was on a business trip in another city during the Christmas season. He was looking forwards to celebrating Christmas with his wife and three children. He then prayed and asked God help him get to the airport on time so that he could fly home and be with them."

That same man caught a taxi cab four hours before his plane departed. Unfortunately, on way to the airport his taxi cab had engine trouble and it would not run. As a result, the man could not get to the airport on time and he ended up missing his flight.

The man was very upset because he would not be able to celebrate Christmas with his wife and children that year." "That same day, that same man was forced to rent a hotel room near the airport. He did not understand why God had not answered his prayer." "The following day, that same man was watching the news on his hotel TV. He was shocked when he heard that the plane meant for him had exploded in mid-air, and that everyone on board was killed. Then the man thanked God for his intervention." "Finally." He said. "During the 1950's there were three teenage girls who decided to start smoking cigarettes. Unfortunately, one girl could not because she had a smoke allergy. She prayed and she asked God to make her smoke allergy go away, so that she could smoke cigarettes just like her two friends did. She never understood why God never answered her prayer. Thirty years later, she was healthy and strong while her two old friends were dead from lung cancer."

Jesus smiled at her. "The Father will always answer your prayers Sandra, though not always the way that we want him to. He knows what is best for us, even though at the time we may disagree with him." Sandra changed to subject yet again. "What about animals? Where do animals go when they die?" "There are animals in the next life." He confirmed. "The Bible says that the lion will lie down with the lamb, and in Heaven, all animals live in peace and harmony with one another." "Then what about bugs?" She asked. "Do bugs have souls or do they just die?"

Jesus though for a moment before he replied. "In truth Sandra, insects do have souls. Though they have "lesser" souls." "Then are there bugs in Heaven?" She asked. Jesus shook his head. "I'm afraid not." Sandra changed the subject again. "When you were being made to suffer during your crucifixion, were you ever tempted to harm the people who were causing you pain?" Jesus frowned and shook his head. "In a way. You must understand that when I first walked the Earth, I was half human. I also told people to never seek revenge on others." "Why is that?" Asked Sandra. Jesus took in a deep breath before replying. "Because It is only human nature to want to hurt someone who has hurt you first."

"If you were to watch enough action movies you would see that quite often the villain wrongs the hero. Say the villain kills the hero's friend, the hero's brother or the hero's partner. In the end of the movie the hero finds a way to kill the villain, and everyone lives happily ever after. That's fantasy. In reality, after the hero murders the villain, the hero will be arrested by the police, charged with murder, and will spend the rest of his life in prison. That never happens in the action movies, does it? In truth getting revenge on people usually makes things worse, and as far as the law is concerned, you're not allowed to get revenge. "Then did you ever forgive your disciples for abandoning you?" She asked. "Of course." Replied Jesus smiling. Sandra spoke again. "Then did you forgive Judas?" Jesus had a blank expression on his face. "Yes, but it wasn't easy." Jesus glanced at his digital watch, then he stood upright. "It was nice talking to you Sandra, but now my time is up and now I must go. Thesecond holy man will arrive shortly."

Sandra held out her hand, touching his arm, feeling his warmth pass through her body. "Must you leave so soon?" "I'm afraid so." Replied Jesus. Sandra looked up at him. "Will you and I ever meet or speak again?" Jesus looked down at her. "Not in this life." He replied. Then Jesus smiled and they shook each other's hands. Then Jesus turned. He walked up the hallway and he disappeared around the corner of the hallway. Sandra sat there thinking about what she had just been told. Thenshe patiently waited for the next holy man.

Chapter 4

Sandra had been waiting on the wide wooden bench for three minutes now, watching students walk past her in both directions. One minute later an Arab man walked down the hallway and up to her. He wore an expensive black suit. He was clean shaven and wore two gold rings and an expensive gold watch, and he had a slightly darker skin tone than Jesus did. Sandra looked up at him. "Are you the next Holy Man?" He smiled down at her. "Of course, and my name is Mohammed." He said, shaking her hand. He then sat down beside her and made himself comfortable on the wide wooden bench. "I created the world religion people call Islam. Have you ever heard of me before?" Sandra nodded. "Yes. I know a handful of things regarding Islam. My professor had mentioned you before."

Mohammed smiled. "Excellent. Most people that live in North America know next to nothing about the religion I created. Now I will teach you all about Islam and answer all of your questions." "Then let's get started." Said Sandra. "Then it's true that Allah is the Muslim name for God?" "Of course." He replied. "God has many names. Something you will understand that by the end of the day." "Then how did you start Islam?" Asked Sandra. "I was born in the year 570 into The Quaraysh Tribe, in a place known as Mecca." He happily explained. "I spent my youth as a merchant. And I was an only child with no brothers or sisters. My mother died when I was only six years old, and my father passed away before I was born, I never knew him. Then I was raised by my grandfather. Though sadly he died two years later. Then my uncle who was a camel merchant took on the role of my father. When I was twenty-five. I got married to a woman named Khadijah who was much older than I was, and together we produced several children."

"One night. I was fasting and mediating inside a cave in a place called Mount Hira when I was in my forties. It was then I was visited by the Archangel Gabriel. Gabriel told me that Allah himself had chosen me to be his latest messenger and prophet. Then the entire Koran appeared in my mind, and I continued receiving revelations for the rest of my life. That event would later be called The Night of Destiny." "Why did God choose you?" Asked Sandra. He smiled at her. "Because Allah found me to be most worthy. I was deeply religious, and because Allah thought that I was wise and fair."

He continued. "Then I traveled all over Arabia, telling people that there was only one true God whom everyone must pray to. I also told people to abandon their false gods and idols, and that everyone must pray to this new unseen and invisible God. And over the years I wrote down the entire Koran." "Eventually

I traveled to a place called Midia. Where I erected my very first Mosque. I also invented the rules that all Muslims were to pray five times a day. At dawn, noon, late afternoon, sunset, and nightfall. And more than a few Muslims carry around special mats that they use to pray with." "Is there a Muslim Hell?" Asked Sandra. "Of course, there is." Confirmed Mohammed. "And we call it Jahannam." "But Jesus spoke to me of angels." She said. "If angels exist why is it I've never seen one?" Mohammed shook his head. "Because the only time that you can see an angel is when it wants you to." "Why were you mediating and fasting for in a cave?" Asked Sandra, changing the subject. "It was a common thing to do in my time period and part of the world." He replied. "Where does the word "Islam" come from?" She asked. "When translated the word Islam means "One who submits himself to Allah." Confirmed Mohammed. Sandra sat there silently for a few seconds before speaking again. "Do people still worship false gods in our day and age?" "I hope not." Replied Mohammed Sandra changed the subject. "Why doesn't God just create onereligion instead of many?"

"For the same reason we all don't drive the same cars, eat the same food, wear the same clothes, or listen to the same music." He replied. "People are different, as a result people found all over the world choose to worship Allah in their own way. Most major world religions are praying to the same person, they are only doing it in their own way. Religion is important. It encourages people to be good and do good. If there was no such thing as religion man's world would be a very dark place. And it is always best that someone take comfort in religion instead of drugs, and alcoholic drinks." "Tell me more about the Koran." She requested. Mohammed nodded. "The Koran is the Muslim Bible. When translated It means "That which should be read." "Then it's true that Muslims dislike Jesus?" Asked Sandra. "Not really." He replied, shaking his head. "We Muslims believe that Jesus was only a prophet and not the son of God, and Jesus's name appears a handful of times in the Koran."

He continued. "You must understand, that in Christianity and the Bible there are quite a few mistakes and misinterpretations." "Such as?" She asked. "Well for starters." He said. "The way that Jesus Christ is depicted in artwork is for the most part wrong." "In artwork, Jesus is almost always depicted as a European, a Caucasian, and a white man with long flowing brown hair and a full beard." He said. "You see Sandra, Jesus didn't come from Europe. Jesus came from Palestine, and people who come from Palestine don't look like that. In truth they have a slightly darker skin tone." Sandra recalled from earlier that Jesus had a slightly darker skin tone.

He kept going. "Many people think that in the book of Genesis after Eve had been tempted by the snake in the Garden of Eden that she had bitten into an apple. If you were to read The Book of Genesis closely enough, you might see that according to The

Bible, Eve bit into a fruit, in the entire book of Genesis the word apple was never used." Mohammed continued. "The famous painting of the last supper is wrong. The painting depicts Jesus and his twelve disciples all eating their dinner at one long table. Eating dinner at one long table is a European custom, not Palestinian. In truth, during the last supper their dinner table was really "U" shaped, and Jesus and his twelve disciples were actually laying on their stomachs as opposed to sitting in chairs." "Another misinterpretation is that when Jesus was born in a manger that he was surrounded by farm animals. In truth, there were none. And Jesus was not an only child, he did have brothers and sisters."

He continued. "In artwork, angels are almost always depicted as white people wearing long robes. They usually have long flowing hair and two wings on their backs. Real angels don't look anything like that. In truth angels are bizarre looking. Quite a few angels have numerous heads while others are covered from head to foot with eyeballs, while other angels have different animal heads." Sandra was confused. "Then if angels look bizarre what do demons really look like?" Mohammed paused for a second before he replied. "Real demons are a grotesque cross between man and animal." "Then do real angels even have wings?" She asked. "It depends on the angel." He replied. "Some angels have wings while others have none. Though some angels have six wings. Two on their backs, two on their wrists, and two on their ankles." He continued. "One of the ten commandments is misinterpreted. "Though shall not kill." You see Sandra, killing somebody in war is not a sin and killing someone in self defense is not a sin, but killing someone for personal reasons is. So, in truth, the commandment is not "Though shall not kill." It is "Though shall not murder."

He moistened his lips before he continued. "Christmas is probably celebrated on the wrong day." "Why is that?" Asked Sandra. "Because." He said. "The Bible does not give Jesus's exact date of birth. So in the year 330 AD Pope Julius decided that Christmas should be celebrated on December the twenty-fifth." Sandra wished that she could have asked Jesus when he was born. "There is more." He said. "In the Bible in the book of Exodus and Revelations, the Bible speaks of water turning into blood. That is another misinterpretation. In truth the water turned red because it was infested with a disease called Anthrax, not because it turned into blood."

He continued. "There is another misinterpretation. When the Bible was first translated into English over a thousand years ago from another language, the word "many" was confused with the word "forty." So in the story of Noah's Ark, it rained for many days and many nights, not forty, and Jesus fasted in the desert for many days and many nights, not forty." "Also, when Christ first walked the Earth, he was not called Jesus. In truth people really called him "Yoshawa." Though over time his name slowly changed to Jesus, and the real Jesus never had long flowing hair. Jesus was a carpenter by trade, and long flowing hair would have only gotten in his way."

"If you were to look at the ceiling of the Sistine Chapel, you might notice that Michelangelo painted Allah as some old wise looking European man who has a long flowing gray beard, long flowing gray hair, wears a long robe and sits on a throne. Give me a break." He said. "I cannot tell you what Allah looks like, but I can tell you that he doesn't look like that." "Then why is Jesus depicted in artwork the way he is?" Asked Sandra.

Mohammed acknowledged her question. "Hundreds of years ago, the great painter Michelangelo wanted to paint a picture of Jesus Christ onto the ceiling of the Sistine Chapel. The problem was that Jesus's physical description was never given mentioned anywhere in the Bible. As a result, Michelangelo used his uncle who had long brown hair and a full beard. And that image has remained to this day." He moistened his lips before resuming. "Last of all, the way that Satan is depicted in artwork is wrong. The Devil is often drawn as a person with red skin, horns on his head, and sometimes has two bat wings on his back. Nowhere in the Bible or Koran is Satan described as looking like that." "You must understand." Said Mohammed. "As far as Islam is concerned, there are quite a few ignorance's." "Quite a few ignorant people say that all Muslim women are forced to wear veils." He said. "That is false. Many Muslim women refuse to wear veils. On the other hand, all Muslim women are expected to dress in a humble way. In a Muslim country a woman does not walk down the street wearing a bikini." "Many people seem to think that only Arabs are Muslims. That is also untrue. We Muslims can be found all over the world." "Many people think that those who practice Islam always have arranged marriages. That is also untrue." "Ignorant people think that real Islam promotes violence and hatred against others. It does not. Those who seek to hurt and harm others are considered an enemy of Islam."

"Many ignorant people think that all Muslims suppress their women. We do not. The Koran says that men and women are both equals and that all women are meant to be treated with dignity and respect." "Last of all." He said. "A Jihad is not a holy war. When translated the word Jihad really means "Struggle." Sandra changed the subject. "What is an Imam?" "An Imam is the name of an Islamic priest." He replied. Sandra shifted her seat on the bench in order to make herself more comfortable. "What do Muslims believe what happens when they die?" "We believe in final judgement, similar to what Christian's believe." He confirmed. "Judgement that results in either a Heaven or a Hell." "What do you think of Jesus?" She asked, changing the subject again.

"Jesus died over five hundred years before my birth." He replied. "Though in Heaven we have spoken. If you were to read The New Testament, you would see that Jesus did not keep in the company of rich, famous or powerful people. He always kept in the company of the outcasts, the people who no one cared about." "Then what is it like inside a Muslim church?" She asked. "I've never been inside one before." He happily explained. "A Muslim church is called a "Mosque" Sandra. All mosques have a wide-open area inside where all Muslims gather to pray and worship Allah. The entire service is done on our knees, unlike Christians who sit on wooden benches like Christians. And we always remove our foot ware when in the prayer area as sign of respect to Allah, and all women are made to sit in a different section than the men." "Do any mosques have statues of you inside?" She asked.

Mohammed shook his head. "Not at all. When I first walked the Earth, I told people to never bow down to idols or statues. As a result you will find no statues of myself or anyone inside any mosque

anywhere." "Earlier you mentioned Mecca." Sandra asked. "Where can it be found?" "Mecca is an Arabic city that can be found in the high desert plateau near the Red Sea in Saudi Arabia." He replied. "All Muslims are strongly encouraged to travel there at least once in their lifetimes." "You call that a haji, right?" Asked Sandra.

Mohammed was impressed. "Excellent Sandra. "You've been paying attention to your professor." He stood, stretched his arms and glanced at his watch. "Well, my time here is up Sandra, and now I must go."

Sandra was saddened by this. "Must you go so soon?" "I'm afraid so." He replied. "The next holy man will arrive shortly. ho he is will be for you to find out." Then the two of them shook hands. Sandra watched Mohammed. He walked down the crowded hallway and around the corner and out of sight.

Chapter 5

After talking to Jesus and Mohammed, Sandra was deep in thought. It was then a third well-dressed man approached the bench two minutes later. He was shaved bald, and had a kind face. His skin tone was a bit lighter than Mohammed. Though Sandra was not sure of his nationality or his age. She looked up at him. "Are you the next holy man?" He smiled back at her and extended his right hand, and they both shook. "Indeed, and you may call me Buddha." "Awesome!" Exclaimed Sandra. "You're the one who created Buddhism?" "You are correct." He replied warmly. "Now I will now teach you all about Buddhism and answer all of your questions." He then sat down beside Sandra on the wooden bench. Sandra looked at him and cut to the chase "How did you create Buddhism?"

Buddha took in a deep breath before replying. "I was born and raised a prince in a small country known as Lumai that is now called Nepal, five hundred years before the birth of Jesus, in a small kingdom found below the Himalayan Foothills, and my father was chief of the Shakya Clan." "Nepal is a very small country that can be found to the north of India. Most people in the world have never heard of it, and even fewer people could ever find it on a world map." "When my mother the queen was expended, one night she had a dream. In that dream she foresaw that her son would become a great holy man one day. After being born my mother named me Siddhartha. Though sadly she died when I was seven. During my youth I was raised as a prince. I was taught archery, wrestling, sword fighting, swimming and running."

He continued. "My Father the king did not want me to grow up and become a great holy man. If such a thing happened, I would be forced to abandon my royalty and there wouldn't be anyone left to carry on our family name. My father feared that if I was ever exposed to evil or human suffering that I would leave all of my royal duties behind and abandon my home forever. So, he ordered his servants to all shield me from all suffering and evil. He also forbode me to ever leave my palace. When I matured, I married a woman called Gopa, and we produced a son together. In all my life I had never left my palace grounds." "When I was nineteen, I went against my father's wishes, and I left my palace in a horse drawn carriage with my charioteer for the very first time in order to see the real world for myself. I then saw four things that forever changed me. First, I saw a very old man, then I saw a very sick man, a dead corpse that was being taken away to be burnt, and then a wandering holy man. At that moment I understood how much pain, suffering, and injustice there was in this world. Then I knew what I was meant to do. I left everything behind, including my wife and son. I then changed my name to Buddha, shaved my head, put on simple clothing, and rid myself of all of my material possessions. Then I spent the next forty-five years traveling and preaching." "Why did you shave your head?" Asked Sandra. He happily explained. "It is a way of being humble." "Why did you change your name to Buddha?" Asked Sandra. "The name Buddha means "Enlightened One." He replied. "And Buddhism stresses deep respect for all life and creation. We don't evenstep on insects."

Sandra made another odd face. "You guys are afraid to step on a ant? That's stupid. Nobody cares if you step on an ant." Buddha looked sympathetic. "The ant cares, and ants are living things. Buddhists are taught to respect all forms of life, no matter how small it may be, just because a life form is small does not make it insignificant, and there is no shame in respecting life." Sandra thought for a second before asking her next question. "Then if I squash some cockroach that has made a home in my house. Am I going straight to Hell?" Buddha shook his head. "No. Killing a cockroach that infests yourhome is not a sin. Cockroaches can spread disease. So can mice, flies, mosquitos, and rats. Killing such creatures that infest your home is nota sin, it is self defense. The Creator understands that, and killing an insect for no good reason is not a sin either."

He continued. "When I was a child in Nepal, I had my own sleeping chamber. One day I noticed that some little spider had spun a web above my bed. All the time that spider lived there I never disturbed it.

Most people would kill a spider that spun a web a home above their bed. I refused. That little spider was trying to survive. It had as much right to life as I did. And everything thing in nature serves a purpose in itself." Sandra made another odd face. "Then if everything in nature serves a purpose, why does God create mosquitoes?" He explained. "Mosquitoes are a food source for birds, fish, turtles, frogs, dragonflies, spiders, and tadpoles." "Then why does God create cockroaches?" She asked. Buddha smiled at her. "Cockroaches help to recycle decay. They also help to get rid of dead plants, dead animals, and animal waste." Sandra spoke again. "Then why does God create fly maggots?" "Fly maggots are important." He said. "They help to dispose of excrement and decaying waste." "Like Islam, there are a few ignorance's regarding Buddhism." He said, changing the subject.

"Many people seem to think that all Buddhists are vegetarians. Most Buddhists are not. And as far as Buddhism is concerned, there is nothing wrong in eating meat, and even I enjoyed eating meat when I first walked the Earth." "Lots of people seem to think that all Buddhists meditate. Most do not." "Many people also think that all Buddhists are pacifists. That is also false. A Buddhist will gladly rise up to defend his land, his country and his people." "Some people also think that the Dali Lama is the Buddhist version of the Pope. He is not. The Dali Lama only represents a branch of Buddhism." Sandra changed the subject. "What do Buddhists believe happens after death? Do you guys believe in an afterlife or do you believe in reincarnation?" "We believe in both." He replied. "Buddhists are taught that everyone goes through constant rebirth until they reach ultimate enlightenment that some people might call Heaven. This state of ultimate truth is called Nirvana. We make spiritual progress with each new life. This goes against the Christian or Muslim belief where your soul faces judgement after death then gets sent to either Heaven or Hell."

Sandra spoke again. "Then do Buddhists believe in a Devil?" "Not really." Replied Buddha. "Then what is a Karma?" Asked Sandra. "Karma is what determines our position in the next life." He said. "It is a record of your sins. A tally sheet of good and bad deeds that follows you throughout your life." "Buddhists believe that we all come back to Earth until we learn the lessons that they need. We call this the wheel of life." Buddha changed the subject again. "Far too many people in this world are obsessed with great riches. Because those people think if they are rich then they will lead a perfect happy life." He said. "Real life doesn't work that way, and in the end, rich people have problems, just like everyone else in the world. Money can't buy happiness, and some of the most miserable people in the world are the richest. Everyone gets frustrated with their lives at some point in time and rich people are no exception. People are always looking for the quick fast easy way to get rich. There is no quick fast easy way to get rich. If there was everybody would be rich." He continued. "Many people seem to think that all movie stars lead perfect, happy, glamorous lives. They don't. In fact, movie stars really lead very stressful lives.""How come?" Asked Sandra.

He happily explained. "Let's say that there is some big-name movie star, and he is eating dinner in a crowded restaurant, and people in the restaurant recognize him." "Those people will all get up and surround him. People will attempt to touch him, shake his hand, take his picture, and get his autograph, and that happens every time he goes out in public. That can be more stressful than you might think, and just because someone is rich and famous does not necessarily mean that they have an easy life. You might think that those movie stars would be happy with all their money and fame, and in the end, they're not." Buddha changed the subject again. "Some people say that there is honor in war. I strongly disagree." "Say that you are in the army, and one day you are sent off to war. And during the war you get a bullet lodged in your stomach, and then you end up dying a very slow, very painful, very agonizing death on the battlefield. Where is the honor in that?"

He continued. "Say that you are in the army and during the war both of your legs get severely wounded. And the only way that the doctors can save your life is to have both of your legs amputated. Then you end up living the rest of your life without any legs. Where is the honor in that? "Last of all." He said. "Let's say that you go to war, and one day during the war you take another man's life. Then you learn that the man whom you just killed has a wife and three children. Where is thehonor in that?"

Buddha changed the subject again. "The reason that all religions encourage non materialism is because attachment to material objects will only hinder your spiritual growth. Far too many people in this world are obsessed with owning fancy cars, big houses, and great amounts of money. You see Sandra, all of the millionaires and billionaires in the world all have the same thing in common. They are all going to die one day, and all their money isn't going to change that. Your body is just a temporary shell for your soul. Everyone dies, one way or another, sooner or later, everybody. There are no exceptions. The Creator puts us here on Earth in order to learn and grow, not to see how much stuff we can buy, and the Creator is more pleased with someone who gives money to charity because it is the right thing to do as opposed to someone who only gives money to charity in front of the media." "People who dedicate their lives to mediation and prayer are the smart ones." He said. "They understand that there is more to life than just this world. Many people think that having great riches will bring them a perfect happy life, though real life doesn't work like that. And the afterlife is far better than this one." "Don't Buddhists have a holy book or Bible?" Asked Sandra. Changing the subject. "Of course, we do." He replied. "We call it The Sutra. My followers wrote it down shortly after I had died. It holds all my teachings." "Let me tell you something else." He said. "If you perform an act of kindness to someone, if that person gets a chance, they will do something kind back to you. And if you do something really mean to someone, if that person gets a chance, they will do something mean back to you." That made a lot of sense too. "Is there any more of your wonderful philosophy that you can tell me?" Asked Sandra smiling.

Buddha smiled back at her. "It really doesn't take much courage to beat up on someone that is smaller and weaker than you are. There never was a good war or bad peace. Anyone can be kind if they choose to be. Sometimes people have a reason for being the way they are, and nobody can give you honesty and nobody can take it away." "I will always remember that." Replied Sandra. "What happened to your wife and son in the end?" He happily explained. "My wife became a nun and my son became a monk."

Buddha stood up and stretched. "Well Sandra, my time is up. And the next holy man will be here shortly. I'm afraid that I must go now. I hope the best for you and your book report." Buddha smiled and shook her hand, he then turned and walked down the university hallway, around the corner and eventually out of sight. Sandra then patiently waited for the next holy man.

Chapter 6

Sandra had been seated on the bench for another two minutes. It was then a man wearing a long back overcoat, black pants, and a black hat approached her. This man was Jewish. Sandra had seen other Jewish men wearing similar clothing in the past. This man was in his mid-thirties. He also had curly black hair and a long curly black beard. She wondered how he kept cool in the summer heat. He smiled and shook Sandra's hand. "Hello there Sandra. My name is Abraham." He said smiling. "And I am the Father of Judaism I am here to teach you all about Judaism and answer all any questions you may have about it." "Then how did you start Judaism?" Asked Sandra.

"Four thousand years ago I was the very first Jew. I originally lived in Iraq, in an ancient city known as Mesopotamia." He explained. "And I was a nomad that lived in the Judean desert. When I was old, Yahweh appeared to me in a dream. He showed me a magnificent country and he told me to journey there. That country would later be called Israel. In this promised land Yahweh also promised me that I would become a great leader. Yahweh also told me that one day my people would become a great nation. And I was the very first person ever to preach about the existence of one supreme God. I told people to turn away from all of their idols and false gods." Sandra knew that Yahweh was the Jewish word for God. Sandra changed the subject. "The Bible and Koran also speaks of false gods. I don't understand, who were the false gods?" "You must understand." Said Abraham. "Five thousand years ago there was no such thing as one supreme God. Different countries, different cultures, and different peoples all over the world prayed and worshipped various gods, spirits and deities." "Then what did the ancient gods look like?" She asked. "It depends on the culture." Replied Abraham. "The spirits whom the Native Americans worshiped looked like what you or I might find odd looking. The Aztec gods from ancient Mexico looked like what you or I might call monsters. The gods of ancient Egypt were sometimes a cross between man and animal, while the gods of ancient Greece and ancient Japan were human looking." "Then where did the ancient gods come from?" Asked Sandra.

Abraham shook his head. "People nowadays aren't sure. Though the ancient humans did claim that their gods were beings who came down from the sky." Sandra changed the subject again. "You just told me that the gods of ancient Egypt were sometimes a cross between man and animal. Mohammed told me that demons were a cross between man and animal." Abraham corrected her. "Some of the gods of ancient Egypt were a cross between man and animal, though not in an evil or grotesque manner." "Then whatever happened to the ancient gods?" Asked

Sandra. "Where are they now?" "The world changed and a new age of one supreme God emerged." He replied. "People stopped praying to them and over time they were forgotten about." "Then why do Jews call themselves Jews?" She asked.

He happily explained. "The name Jew originated from a person in Jewish history. His name was Judah." "What does Judaism say happens to people when they die?" She asked, changing the subject yet again. "Like Christianity and Islam, we believe in final judgement. Resulting in either a Heaven or a Hell." He replied. Sandra thought for a second before asking her next question. "What is the Jewish Bible called?" "It is called "The Torah." He replied. "When translated, the word Torah means "teachings" in Hebrew." "Isn't Torah the name of a car?" "That's Taurus," Said Abraham, correcting her. "Was Moses a real person?" She asked. "Of course, he was." Replied Abraham. "Then will I meet Moses today?" She asked.

Abraham shook his head. "I'm afraid not. Moses was never a holy man. Moses only delivered my people from servitude from the Ancient Egyptians, and he led my people to the promised Land. Though he did not create any world religion." Sandra changed the subject. "The other holy man told me that when we die our souls leave our bodies. What part of our body does our soul reside?" He cleared his throat before speaking. "Your soul is not inside your body Sandra. It surrounds your body as an invisible aura." "Then what is God like?" She asked. Abraham smiled at her. "He is many things. He is a very compassionate God, a gentle loving God, and a very wise and forgiving God, he is always fair, slow to anger, and he is far beyond what you or Imight call a life form."

Abraham continued. "Say that you and your family are starving, if you were to pray to him, he will never ignore you. He will not make you or your family super rich, on the other hand he won't let you and your family starve either, and at times he even finds things amusing." Sandra paused for a moment before she replying. "God has a sense of humor?" "Of course, he does." Replied Abraham, smiling. Sandra made another odd face. "But God having a sense of humor was never mentioned anywhere in the Bible." "That's true." He said. "On the other hand, Alexander the Great and Abraham Lincoln also had a sense of humor too, though you won't read about that in too many history books, will you?"

He continued. "If you were to look down at an ant you would see that it is a very inferior life form. A simple ant could never begin to comprehend who or what you are or the world around it. Compared to Yahweh you are less than an ant. As a result, you can never begin to comprehend who he is or the wonders he performs." "Does God still perform wonders in this day and age?" She asked. "Everyday." Replied Abraham. "A sunrise, the birth of a child." "I remember watching a TV documentary about Israel. It showed many Jews that were all praying at some giant stone wall." Said Sandra, changing the subject.

"Why is that done?"

Abraham thought to himself for a second before replying. "You speak of the Wailing Wall, or the Temple Mount. To us Jews the Temple Mount is considered as a sacred holy site, and it is the last remaining section of the second temple." "Then what do you call Jewish churches and Jewish priests?" She asked. "Synagogues," Replied Abraham. "We call them Synagogues. When translated the word Synagogue means "Place of assembly." And we call Jewish priests Rabbi's." When translated the word "Rabbi" means "teacher" "What about the Holocaust?" Asked Sandra. "Why didn't God intervene and stop the Holocaust from happening?" "In a way he did." Replied Abraham. "Perhaps if Yahweh had not intervened, perhaps the bad guys would have won the Second World War, and if the bad guys had won the Second World War, right now you might be oppressed, or you might even be a slave."

Abraham then stood and stretched his arms. "Well, my time is up, and now I must go. Good luck on your report." He smiled and shook her hand. He then walked down the hallway around a corner and out of sight. Then Sandra patiently waited for the next holy man.

Chapter 7

After sitting on the bench for another two minutes, an East Indian man walked up to her. He had a different skin tone than Mohammed or Jesus. He also had short black hair he was also well dressed.

After shaking each other's hands, he sat down beside her on the bench and he made himself comfortable. "Hello there Sandra. My name is Shiva, and I am the next holy man whom you will speak with today." He said. "I have assumed human form so I can speak with you."

"I am one millions of different Hindu gods." He said. "Hinduism is over five thousand years old, and it is the oldest world religion that is still in practice."

Sandra contradicted him. "But Jesus told me that Voodoo was around six thousand years before his birth."

"That's true." He confirmed. "On the other hand, Voodoo is not a major world religion."

Sandra spoke again. "A long time ago I saw a TV documentary about Hinduism. I hope that helps some of my questions." "Every little bit does." He said, smiling at her.

Sandra got to the point. "How did you create Hinduism?" She asked.

Shiva shook his head. "I didn't. Unlike most modern-day religions Hinduism does not have a single founder like Jesus, Mohammed, Buddha, Abraham or Guru Nanak. Hinduism began slowly and gradually over a very long period of time. Hinduism dates back so far that people aren't even sure when it all began. Hindus pray to millions of different gods, and deities. We do not believe in a Heaven/Hell the same way other modern religions do. Hindus believe in rebirth and reincarnation. Hindus are told that if they do well in life that their souls get reborn into a higher level of existence. The fate of their souls depends on the choices that they may have made during their time on Earth. Those who have lived a dishonest life will get reincarnated into a lower life form like a rat or a worm. Hindus are taught that if they perform well in life, and get brought back into the world enough times, that they will eventually gain a higher level of existence called Moksha. Moksha is similar to what some people might call Heaven."

"Don't Hindu's have a chief god?" Asked Sandra.

"Of course, we do." He replied. "And his name is Brahman. Hindus are told that Brahman is everywhere and in everything." "Then what is your purpose?" She asked.

Shiva exhaled hard before replying. "I am the god of procreation and reproduction. I am also responsible for life and death."

"A handful of the millions of deities worshiped by Hindu's look like what you might call monsters." He also confirmed. "For example, the goddess Kali has blue skin. She also has ten arms, ten legs, a long tongue that hangs out of her mouth, and she wears as a necklace that ismade out of several human skulls."

Sandra made another odd facial expression. "Then Hindu's pray tomonsters?"

Shiva grew very serious and he looked Sandra in the eye. "Let me tell you something about monsters Sandra. You humans are a very cruelspecies. You pour poisonous chemicals into the rivers, lakes, and oceans, you experiment on animals, you put animals in cages, you burn down the rain forest, you pollute the air, you hunt animals for sport, you kill insects for no reason, you hunt animal species to extinction, you leave your garbage and waste in the middle of forests, and you are cruel to animals. Perhaps you humans are the greatest monsters of them all."

Sandra changed the subject yet again. "I don't understand. Why do Hindu's pray to spirits? Jesus said that spirits were the souls of people that were in limbo."

Shiva raised his finger and he corrected her. "No. Jesus told you that "ghosts" were the souls of people that were in limbo, not spirits." Sandra was bewildered. "There's a difference?"

"Of course, there is." He replied. "Spirits are supernatural beings that exist, while ghosts are the souls of people who are in limbo, though ghosts and spirits are often confused with one another."

"Then are there evil spirits?" She asked. "Of course, there are." He replied.

Sandra was confused again. "Then all evil spirits are grotesque looking monsters?"

"Not neccessarily." He replied. "It is only human arrogance to assume that just because something is evil that it has to be ugly. That's not always true. Evil has the power to look beautiful. It is also human arrogance to think that The Earth belongs to man, it does not. Man belongs to The Earth."

"But I've never seen a spirit before. "Said Sandra. "What do spiritsreally look like?"

"It depends on the spirit." He said. "And the only time that youcan see one is when it wants you to."

"Jesus told me the same thing regarding angels." Said Sandra."How do you explain that?"

"You must understand Sandra, there are some things that exist that human eye just cannot see." He replied. "You can hear the wind, and you can feel the wind but you can't see the wind."

"Then what is a spirit's true form?" She asked. "Orbs of light." He replied.

Sandra changed the subject again. "I recall hearing somethingabout cows and Hinduism."

"To Hindu's cows are considered sacred animals." He

said. "Hindus believe that spirits reside inside the cows, and that praying to them will bring them happiness and peace, and in India all cows have free roam."

"Then what happens if someone kills one of the cows?" She asked.

He frowned. "Then that person will be severely punished, even if it was an accident."

Sandra moistened her lips before speaking again. "You said earlier that you had assumed human form in order to speak to me. If that's true, what do you really look like?"

"In my true form I come with four arms and blue skin." He said as he glanced across the crowded hallway. "It would be very inappropriate to assume my true form in these surroundings. It would shock people, and my skin is blue because in Hinduism the color blue is associated with holiness."

"That also makes sense." She said. "Don't Hindu's have some kind of holy book?"

He nodded. "Of course, we do. We call it The Vedas," and a Hindu church is called a Madir."

"Who is the character with has the three faces?" She asked. "You speak of Brahma," He replied.

Sandra was confused again. "Your chief god has three faces?"

He corrected her. "No, the person with the three faces is <u>Brama</u> not <u>Braman</u>."

Sandra repeated her question. "Why does Brama have three faces."

"After creating woman, he fell in love with one." Explained Shiva. "He loved her so much that he put two extra faces on his head in order to see her at all times."

"Then who is the person with the four arms and the elephant head?" Asked Sandra.

"That is my son Ganesha." Replied Shiva.

"Why on Earth does he have four arms and an elephant head?"

She asked, with another odd look on her face.

"There is a story to support that." He said. "A long time ago I returned from a long journey. When I did, I found a stranger at my door. This made me angry, so I had him beheaded. I was then shocked to learn that the person whom I just executed was my own son Ganesha. Desperate to make amends. I cut the head off of a passing elephant and put it onto his shoulders. From then on, he had the head of an elephant, including four arms that he had inherited from his father."

Sandra thought for a moment before she spoke again. "Then what is the difference between a Hindi, and a Hindu?"

"Good question," He said smiling. "Hindu are a people, while Hindi is a language. The word Hindu originated from a tribe of people that once lived in

Northern India."

Shiva then glanced at his wrist watch. He then stood upright.

"Well, my time is up Sandra, and now I must go."

"Will I get to meet any holy men from Africa today?" She asked.

Shiva shook his head. "I'm afraid not."

Sandra frowned. "Why is that? And what major world religion can be found in Africa?"

"All world religions can be found in Africa." He replied, smiling.

Shiva and Sandra then shook each other's hands. Shiva then turned and then he walked down the hallway and out of sight. Sandra then patiently waited for the next holy man.

Chapter 8

Sandra was still seated on the bench. She wondered whom she would speak to next. Two minutes later, a second East Indian man walked up to the bench. He had a darker skin tone that Buddha's though lighter than Shiva's. He also wore a brown business suit, a tie, had a black turban on his head, and was a bit plump. He also had a long white beard. He almost reminded Sandra of an East Indian Santa Clause.

The man politely extended his hand. "Hello Sandra. I am the next holy man, and you may call me Guru Nanak," He said.

Sandra silently extended her hand and they shook. She had neverheard of Guru Nanak before.

Guru Nanak sat down beside her and he made himself comfortable on the bench. "I created the world religion called Sikhism." He said. "And I have come to teach you all about my religion and answer all of your questions, and I will be the last holy man that you will speak with today."

"Then you started Sikhism?" Asked Sandra. "How did you do it?"

Nanak would explain. "I was born and raised a Hindu in the year 1469 in section of northern India people call Punjab in a village known as Talwandi. I was an accountant with a wife and two sons."

"One day, when I was in my thirties. I was bathing in a nearby river until I disappeared. Leaving my clothing on the river bank. All of my friends and family feared that I had drown, and that the river had carried my corpse away. In truth, I was with God himself. Three days later I reappeared."

"The very first thing I said was. "There is neither Hindu nor Muslim." God himself had chosen me as his next prophet. I borrowed beliefs from Hinduism and Islam, and I created something totally new that I called Sikhism. Soon after, I was awarded the name Guru as well as a turban. Then I spent the rest of my life traveling and preaching."

He leaned back on the bench and continued. "I then spent the rest of my life traveling all over Saudi Arabia, Tibet, and Sri Lanka. Telling people that there was only one true God who is just, everywhere, and is the greatest Guru of them all. God has no gender and cannot be comprehended by us human beings. I also preached that everyone is equal, black and white, male or female, rich or poor, wise or fool."

"Why were you rewarded a turban?" She asked.

"At one time a turban was a sign of power and respect." He replied. "Over time, all Sikh men adopted the custom. To us Sikhs, a turban is a sign of our faith, and the turbans are also used to hold our long uncut hair."

Sandra made another odd face. "Then doesn't your hair ever startto smell or get dirty?"

He laughed. "We don't wear our turbans when we sleep or when we shower. Just because we keep long uncut hair covered does not mean that we don't care for it."

Sandra changed the subject again. "In the Old Testament, God appeared to people face to face to people like Moses and Job. Does God appear to people face to face in this time period?"

"Not at all." He replied.

"Why is that?" Asked Sandra.

He thought for a moment before replying. "Because out of God's endless wisdom he has decided to no longer directly interfere with the affairs of man. He now prefers to operate from a distance."

Sandra changed the subject yet again. "What does God do with the souls of people who commit suicide?"

Nanak shrugged. "I have no idea. It depends on the

reasons." "Say there is a teenage girl who kills herself because she broke up with her boyfriend, then there is another man that takes his own life because he is mentally ill, while another man commits suicide before his enemies torture him to death. It is for God to judge such people, notme."

"What about assisted suicide?" Asked Sandra. "Is that wrong?"

"Yes, it is." Replied Nanak.

Sandra made another strange face. "But if some person is suffering from a horrible disease that will only kill them, and that person is suffering for no good reason, doesn't that individual have the right to die and end to all of their pain? God of all people must understand that."

Nanak frowned and shook his head. "You see something Sandra, everything that happens to us in our lifetimes happens for a reason, and those people that are suffering are suffering for a reason."

"Let me tell you a little story to explain that." He said. "One day there was a man who had a disease. He was looking for a wise healer with magical healing powers whom he had heard of. The healer was a wise man with a follower. The man eventually found the wise magic healer, and told him all about his disease. He then asked the wise healer to use his magic healing powers and cure him. Then the wise healer refused. Then that man walked away upset and with his head lowered to never be seen again."

"After the man had left, the wise healer's follower asked the wise healer why he did not heal that man. The wise healer told his follower that the man had his disease for a reason, and that that man was suffering for a reason." He had given Sandra much to ponder.

Sandra changed the subject yet again. "Do Sikh's have some kindof Bible or holy book?"

Nanak smiled. "Of course, we do, and we call it the Guru Grath

Sahib."

"Then what do you call a Sikh church?" She asked.

Nanak cleared his throat before replying. "A Sikh temple is called a Gurdwara. The word Gurdwara means "Doorway of The Guru when translated. And like Muslims, we do not wear foot ware in the prayer area. That is considered disrespectful, and when each service ends, everyone gathered shares a large meal together. This is done to show that we are all equal, and that Sikhs are all one big family. The large meal is called a Langar, and it is paid for by donations. And every Sikh temple has a number of Guru pictures adorning its walls."

"What do Sikh's believe happens to them when they

die?" Asked Sandra.

Nanak placed his finger on his temple. "Sikhs believe in what is called Samsara, Sandra. Samsara is the repetitive cycle of birth, life and death, similar to what Hindu and Buddhists believe."

"Then what does the word Sikh mean?" Asked Sandra.

"The word Sikh means "disciples" or "Someone who learns" He confirmed. "A disciple is someone that spreads his master's teachings. And a Sikh mass is held every day unlike Christians who usually attend Chruch on Sundays"

"Then how did you die?" She asked.

Nanak frowned again. "In my time period there were people called Moguls that ruled Northern India. My preaching rubbed them the wrong way, as a result they sent an assassin to get me. The assassin stabbed me in the back and I died as a result. Soon after my death my followers burnt my body. Then I was succeeded by nine other Guru's."

He continued. "We Sikhs also have five commandments. That we are not to harm living beings, not to take what is not given, to avoid improper sexual activity, not to take part in improper speech, and to never use drugs or alcoholic drinks."

Nanak then stood up. He smiled and extended his

hand, and they shook each other's hands. "It was a pleasure speaking with you Sandra.

But my time is up now and I must also go. I hope the best for you and your book report."

Sandra watched Guru Nanak walk away, down the crowded hallway around the corner and eventually out of sight. Students walked past her as if nothing important had happened. No one knew that six holy men had in their presence.

Sandra stood up and stretched. She had been seated on the hard wooden bench for almost an hour. Then she left the university building and returned to her apartment building. Sandra was happy to be walking freely without feeling any pain from her left knee. When she reached her apartment building, she caught the elevator to her second- floor apartment. She opened her door using her key card, she then closed and locked the door behind her. Then she sat in front of her desktop computer and turned it on. She then started to write her term paper on world religions.

Conclusion

Two weeks later.

Sandra was seated in a lecture hall in her university. The same lecture hall mentioned earlier. Sandra was seated on an upper row. That day she wore a blue blouse and a long black dress that came down to her ankles. Her professor was handing back their book reports.

Sandra smiled as she accepted her paper on world religions. She was even happier when she saw the A+ grade on the cover.

After the lecture was over, Sandra returned to her apartmentbuilding. She was very proud of herself.

When in her apartment she sat on her bed, smiled, and closed her eyes. She prayed to God, and thanked him for sending all six of his holy men to speak with her on her behalf.

After she had finished praying, she dearly wished that she could speak with the six holy men again, though deep down she knew that that would never happen, at least not in this life.

In one week. Sandra would graduate. She had already sent a resume off to a Catholic high school in Edmonton, and she knew that God would help her to get that position.

Graduating university would be a milestone in her life, and her life would never be the same, thanks to the holy men.